AFRICAN DANCE TRENDS

DANCE & FITNESS TRENDS

Tammy Gagne

Mitchell Lane
PUBLISHERS
P.O. Box 196
Hockessin, DE 19707

African Dance Trends
Get Fit with Video Workouts
Line Dances Around the World
Trends in Hip-Hop Dance
Trends in Martial Arts
The World of CrossFit
Yoga Fitness
Zumba Fitness

PUBLISHER'S NOTE: The facts in this book have been thoroughly researched. Documentation of such research can be found on pages 44-45. While every possible effort has been made to ensure accuracy, the publisher will not assume liability for damages caused by inaccuracies in the data, and makes no warranty on the accuracy of the information contained herein.

The Internet sites referenced herein were active as of the publication date. Due to the fleeting nature of some web sites, we cannot guarantee that they will all be active when you are reading this book.

Printing
1 2 3 4 5 6 7 8 9

Library of Congress
Cataloging-in-Publication Data

Gagne, Tammy.
  African dance trends / by Tammy Gagne.
      pages cm. — (Dance and fitness trends)
  Includes bibliographical references and index.
  ISBN 978-1-61228-557-3 (library bound)
  1. Dance—Africa—Juvenile literature.
  2. Physical fitness—Juvenile literature. I. Title.
  GV1705.G34 2015
  793.3196—dc23
                                    2014006928

eBook ISBN: 9781612285979

                                    PBP

Contents

The continent of Africa is rich in its many traditions including music and dance. Each country has its own unique variety of ceremonies and celebrations that utilize these forms of expression. In some villages dance plays a large role in religion. It also marks important milestones for tribe members, both young and old. Dance can honor a person's birth, marriage, or even death.

Some African tribes use dance as part of healing rituals. So-called witch doctors or medicine men may dance around a sick person, chanting or singing words offered for the sake of curing the illness. In South Africa, these traditional healers, called *sangomas*, dance to beating drums at increasing speeds and intensity before collapsing to the ground. Through this ritual the sangomas claim that they can connect to deceased ancestors in order to diagnose a person's past, present, and future. Some even say they can tell a person when and how he or she will die.

In West Africa dance has long been a way that leaders demonstrate their authority. In Nigeria, for example, the king

Introduction

of the Yoruba people once had to prove his leadership ability with a traditional dance. Other community leaders, such as chiefs, would join him in this performance, each with a specific dance that represented his position. Every physically able person within the community was expected to dance at one time or another.

In modern-day Africa, most dances are performed for social reasons. They help the people celebrate their traditional cultures. African dance has also made its way to other continents around the world. Some types of dance have remained unchanged through the years, while others have been further developed in these new lands. Today African dance is also used as a form of physical fitness in many places. The energetic movements of the dancing combined with the pulsing rhythms of drumming help make African dance an enjoyable and effective way for people everywhere to stay in—or to get into—excellent physical condition.

Most African dances that were developed in the Western Hemisphere were a result of the slave trade. Many African slaves relied on dancing and singing to relieve the stress from the horrible experiences they were enduring. The dances retained many traditional movements and rhythms, but some became blended with other dances, resulting in new forms of dance.

Chapter 1
Can't Take That Away

During the sixteenth and seventeenth centuries, millions of men, women, and children from West Africa were captured for the slave trade. These people were then forced against their will to board ships that carried them to the New World. Once there, they were sold as laborers to European settlers. This period in history is often referred to as the Middle Passage. During this horrible process, the African people lost nearly everything that had been familiar to them. They left their homes, their family and friends, and virtually everything else behind. Most of these people would never return to their home continent.

One of the few things that the Europeans could not take away from the African slaves was their culture. These beliefs and practices, including dance, were things the African people carried with them to the New World. Still, the Westerners did their best to force the African people to abandon their ways. Most of the Westerners were very religious. And they thought that their Christian religions were the only beliefs of any importance. Often Africans were not allowed to practice their own religions.

Many white slave owners saw the Africans as uncivilized beings that were more like animals than people. Perhaps this is how people involved with the slave trade convinced themselves that buying and selling human beings was acceptable. Many African people endured horrible treatment as slaves. One of the ways that they dealt with their feelings of sadness and desperation was by holding onto as much of their culture as they could. A big part of this was dance.

STOWAGE OF THE BRITISH SLAVE SHIP 'BROOKES' UNDER THE

REGULATED SLAVE TRADE

Act of 1788.

*Fig 1
Longitudinal Section*

Hold for Provisions Water &c

PLAN OF LOWER DECK WITH THE STOWAGE OF 292 SLAVES

130 OF THESE BEING STOWED UNDER THE SHELVES AS SHEWN IN FIGURE 9 & FIGURE 3.

Store Room

Store Rooms

PLAN SHEWING THE STOWAGE OF 130 ADDITIONAL SLAVES ROUND THE WINGS OR SIDES OF THE LOWER DECK BY MEANS OF PLATFORMS OR SHELVES (IN THE MANNER OF GALLERIES IN A CHURCH) THE SLAVES STOWED ON THE SHELVES AND BELOW THEM HAVE ONLY A HEIGHT OF 2 FEET 7 INCHES BETWEEN THE BEAMS AND FAR LESS UNDER THE BEAMS . *See Fig 1.*

WOMEN   BOYS   MEN

*Fig 6.
Lower tier of Slaves under the Poop.*

Slave ships like this British ship called the *Brookes* carried hundreds of Africans to the New World on each trip. Often the African men, women, and children were so tightly packed that they could barely move during the journey.

Interestingly, the slave traders actually helped preserve the dance culture of the African slaves. The traders did not set out to do this. Instead, they were worried that the long journey across the Atlantic Ocean would weaken the slaves' bodies. If they didn't have exercise, how would the slaves stay strong? If they could not work, the Africans would be useless to the traders. Healthy slaves, on the other hand, would fetch high prices. They dealt with this problem by forcing the captured Africans to dance.

At this time there was no joy involved in the dancing. While traveling to the New World, most of the Africans were kept in horrid conditions below the decks of the ships. It was dark, dirty, and crowded. But for a certain amount of time, the captives were brought to the ships' decks for exercise. They were then made to move in various ways to the beat of a drum, all while chained to one another. This practice was referred to as "dancing the slaves."

The traders also used dance to keep the Africans from giving up on life. Many of them showed signs of serious depression as a result of their capture. The ones who felt the most despair tried to kill themselves to escape their dreadful reality. And to the captors, a dead slave was even more worthless than a weak or sick one.

Despite their self-serving reasons for "dancing the slaves," the traders were keeping African dance alive in the minds and hearts of the African people. Many Africans held onto this part of their culture. It likely helped some of them endure the further cruelty that awaited them on the other side of the ocean.

Many European settlers did not approve of African dance. They saw the ways the Africans moved their bodies as crude and offensive—in complete opposition to the slave owners' Christian beliefs. They would not allow the African slaves to practice their traditional religions, or the dances that these religions included.

Slaves responded by changing their dances to better suit the Europeans. In this way the slaves were able to hold onto at least some of their culture. They replaced movements that the white settlers deemed obscene with dance steps that the Europeans performed in their own forms of dancing. The result was a mixing of these cultures that still exists today in many forms.

Not all the settlers felt so strongly about the Africans' ways of dancing, however. Many French and Spanish slave owners, for example, saw the Africans as merely primitive human beings. They saw dancing as a harmless form of entertainment, not a threat to their own belief systems. Although not all French and Spanish settlers embraced African dance, they didn't see a need to forbid it. They allowed the Africans to hold onto this part of their culture.

Clever slave owners also realized that dance could serve as an incentive for the slaves to work hard. These settlers would allow their slaves to have a night of dancing on the weekend if they got enough work done during the week. With so little else to look forward to in their lives, the slaves valued this rare recreational time.

Over time many European settlers discovered that they enjoyed watching African dance. Some even showed interest in learning it themselves. Performances called minstrel shows, which featured a merging of African and European dance and music, became very popular in the 1830s. In these shows white dancers performed dance moves normally done by blacks. The white performers would wear makeup to darken their faces. At this time blacks did not perform in minstrel shows—with one rare exception.

A black dancer named William Henry Lane went down in history as one of the most talented dancers of the nineteenth century. Although other black dancers performed in many minstrel shows after the Civil War (1861-1865), Lane was appearing in these shows in the 1840s. The talented dancer,

The Old Plantation, a 1780s painting by an unknown artist, shows slaves dancing to banjo music during some rare time away from their work.

also known as Master Juba, even went on tour with an all-white American dance company as its star in the late 1840s.

Many people regard Lane as the father of tap dance. Dancer and choreographer Lane Alexander is one of them. "We absolutely continue to celebrate William Henry Lane's legacy because of what he accomplished and when he accomplished it," Alexander told *The Washington Post*. "Imagine being a black man in the United States in the 1840s, not the best of circumstances. Despite that he excelled. He succeeded. He broke all kinds of barriers."

Other black dancers would follow in Lane's footsteps. They would proudly hold onto their African heritage as they too became pioneers in the field of dance. In the process people everywhere would discover a large variety of African and African-inspired dance forms that would remain popular throughout the world for centuries to come.

Today African dance serves as both a cultural experience and a powerful form of fitness. The movements stretch and strengthen the body while they also calm the mind. For people

William Henry Lane, better known as Master Juba, is seen here in an issue of *The Illustrated London News* from 1848. Lane was a pioneer among African American dancers.

of African descent, African dance can be a fulfilling way to celebrate their heritage. Others too can appreciate the freedom and expression of these exciting pastimes.

A very unique form of African dance that evolved in the New World is capoeira. This dance form began in Brazil as a secret martial art. No one knows for certain whether the dance existed prior to this time or if slaves created it in South America. During the time of slavery, Africans could practice capoeira without their owners knowing its full purpose. Once the skills were perfected, the slaves could then use this dance as a form of self-defense when necessary.

Today capoeira is at once a dance and a sport. But it is rarely violent. As a game, or *jogo*, of capoeira begins, the performers and audience members form a circle, called the *roda*. Music is a key element. The group includes three musicians who start the jogo by playing bowlike instruments called *berimbaus*. Soon other musicians join in. One person beats a drum called the *atabaque* while others shake a tambourine-like instrument called the *pandeiro*. A two-headed bell called the *agogô* and a percussion instrument called the *reco-reco* are also played.

As the music plays, the two competitors enter the circle, often in acrobatic movements that resemble cartwheels. They then engage in a series of strikes that are not intended to land on the other person. Instead, the game is filled with elaborate near-misses, handstands, jumps, and spins. The object is not to defeat the other person by force, but rather with talent. Technically, the jogo ends with no winner. But one competitor may certainly out-perform the other.

Brazil outlawed capoeira in the 1890s, as police increasingly believed that those who played the sport were causing trouble in other ways. People discovered practicing the sport during this time were punished severely. They could even be forced to leave the country for good. Capoeira was legalized in the mid-1930s when a teacher named Mestre Bimba was given permission to open a school by President Getúlio Vargas. The president liked the martial art so much that he declared it a national sport.

Djoniba Mouflet participates in New York City's 2007 West Indian Day Parade as a drummer. The event was created from the modern celebration of carnival in Trinidad and Tobago. But the traditions on which it is based date back thousands of years to the African continent.

Chapter 2
Modern Pioneers

Djoniba Mouflet was born on a tiny island in the eastern Caribbean Sea called Martinique. But when he got older, he studied African dance on two continents. He worked with masters in the African countries of Guinea, Mali, and Senegal. He also trained in the United States at the Dance Theatre of Harlem. Today Mouflet is one of the best-known teachers of West African dance in New York City, where he directs the Djoniba Dance and Drum Centre. It is a job he has had for more than twenty years now.

Mouflet is also the founder and choreographer of Ballet D'Afrique Djoniba. This group performs traditional West African dance and music. Drumming is a big part of many African dance styles. As Mouflet explained to *Dance Magazine*, "In African dance the live music is so important. The lead drummer leads the dance, so you need to teach people how the music relates to the movement. The music and dance are totally intertwined—they are one."

In addition to being a beautiful art form, African dance also delivers a powerful workout to those who perform it. Mouflet has written a book and produced a DVD to teach even more people his dance technique. He named his technique Joneeba, which is the phonetic spelling of his name. Whether you follow along with one of the videos or attend a class in person, you will notice that a Joneeba class begins by warming up the muscles. Mouflet uses a combination of moves from ballet, modern dance, and even yoga to make sure that the dancers' bodies are ready for the moves ahead.

African dance can be an ideal form of physical fitness. Because so many of the movements are quick and intense, this type of dancing can really get the heart pumping. Taking part in African dance can even have a positive effect on a person's mental well-being.

He then breaks down the steps, teaching them one by one. Although the dance looks complicated, nearly anyone can learn Joneeba this way. Once the students have practiced all the steps, they can then put them together in a full dance routine. Of course, you may pick up some of the steps more quickly if you have taken ballet or other dance classes in the past, but this experience isn't necessary.

What makes Joneeba unique is that it allows dancers to control their bodies and be free with them at the same time. Mouflet shared with *Dance Magazine,* "African dance teaches you to become a musical instrument. You have to be on the beat. Every part of your body has to feel like rhythm. Your head, your shoulders, your arms, your hands, your knees, your chest, your hips. If I see an African dancer who really is doing it right, fully, without any music, then it makes me wanna move. It's just like when you hear good music—you know naturally. It also teaches you to let go of your body, instead of controlling it to the end. You can't completely let go because it becomes sloppy. So you learn to let go, but with control."

Another thing that makes Joneeba different from other types of dancing is that it moves the body in ways most people aren't used to. When you take a step to the right, for example, you may move your left arm as you do so. This could feel a bit awkward to a beginner. Mastering this and other moves takes time. Mouflet points out that Joneeba students must be willing to learn and to give 100 percent effort. "You can't just do the same step over and over." He also shared with *Dance Magazine* that many people mistakenly think that African dance is made up of the same moves, "that the step you're learning is the same as it was one thousand years ago. But what you see mostly in the Western world is steps by choreographers in Africa—based, however, on very key principles and traditional rhythms from different tribes."

Like Mouflet, Naomi Fall was not born in Africa. But that didn't stop her from wanting to learn and teach African dance. She had been dancing from a young age, and this style came very naturally to her.

"After growing up in France," she wrote in *Dance Magazine,* "I went to Sarah Lawrence College in New York. While studying there, I took my first West African dance class, which quickly became a passion. . . . I loved the feeling of pure joy and dance high it gave me. I then went to Senegal and Ghana to study ethnomusicology. After graduating in 2009, I went to Bamako, Mali, for six months to study their traditional dances. On good days, when the dancing and the drumming are suddenly magically in sync, it's like deeply rooted flying! The rhythm gets faster and so do your feet, without any effort, you just let yourself go."

More than just a personal pastime, dance became a way for Fall to help others while she lived in Mali. She soon learned that she could use dance as a way of relating to less fortunate young people. As she told *Dance Magazine*, "I taught contemporary dance to a group of street kids living in very precarious situations. After three months, they were transformed. They could trust, laugh with me, and enjoy coming to the sessions. I understood I could make a difference with dance. The artist's responsibility has always meant a lot to me. We are the voices of our societies; our concerns go far beyond ourselves. We can say what others can't, in ways others can't."

In 2011, Fall returned to the United States. But something was missing in her life there. She missed Bamako so much that she returned later that same year. Her passion for African dance had grown into a desire to help people in Mali become professional dancers themselves. Bear in mind that traditional dance performances in this area of the world take place outdoors. Professional dance classes, as we think of them in the US, weren't available there—until now, that is. Fall met up with a fellow dancer and choreographer named Mohamed Coulibaly in Mali. They decided to open a dance studio called GnagamiX. It offers free classes to both adults and children interested in learning contemporary dance.

GnagamiX's first project was a tour that took the group across the Mandé region of Africa. This area is in the south of Mali and continues past its southern and western borders into the surrounding countries. It consists mostly of small villages. Many of the people there didn't even know that contemporary

In Mali, the Dogon people perform different dances for different purposes. The most famous are their ritual funeral dances, which honor the passing of a village elder. Other dances are kept secret from the outside world.

dance existed. "The shows were very exciting," Fall recalled in *Dance Magazine*. "Three hundred people around us were laughing out loud, screaming. Some were scared, then got caught by the dance; some were even dancing with us from their seats. At a talkback in one of the villages, people came to us talking about love, brotherhood, household issues, friendship, the themes they had seen in the piece and appreciated. They thanked us for bringing something new to their lives. What a boost!"

As welcomed as the dance troop felt by the people, teaching dance in this region is not an easy task. A war is now taking place in some cities where terrorists are trying to take over the country. In the process, they are imposing a set of Islamic laws called sharia. Some religious leaders believe that these laws and punishments come directly from God. Fall continues to use dance as a way of helping people in need, however. "I am staying," she declared to *Dance Magazine* readers, "because continuing our work is an act of resistance towards people who believe art is evil. By dancing, we resist their power and build a constructive and creative future."

More and more schools are celebrating dances from all around the world, including those that originated in Africa. In 2013 Point Park University in Pittsburgh, Pennsylvania, hosted a festival that featured a variety of international dance forms. The school's eight dance studios offered students a chance to try Latin, Middle Eastern, Ukrainian, and West African dance. The response to World Cultural Dance Week was overwhelming—the classes were packed full of interested students.

The event was organized by Point Park's Dance Club, which is run entirely by students. The club held raffles and bake sales to make the event happen. Teachers from the Pittsburgh area were brought onto the university campus to teach classes in various styles. Desiree Lee led the West African dance workshop. She began performing African dance professionally in 1992 as part of the Shona Sharif African Dance Ensemble, and has even traveled overseas to dance in the West African country of Senegal.

Kiesha Lalama is the jazz teacher at the university. She told *Dance Magazine,* "Exposing students to world dance is so important. [This week] forces students to step out beyond what they know and it deepens their appreciation of all kinds of dance." Although the school already offers students a wide range of dance styles, Lalama adds that World Cultural Dance Week "shows what else they are hungry for, and they make it happen for themselves."

Christian Warner is a dance major at the school. After taking a variety of the week's classes, he told *Dance Magazine* that each one offered him something different. "West African was very energetic; butoh was very internal. I'm so glad that I got to participate."

Baba Chuck Davis is the founder and artistic director of DanceAfrica. He is seen here introducing DanceAfrica 2013 at the Brooklyn Academy of Music's Howard Gilman Opera House.

Chapter 3
African Queens

For the last twenty years a dance, percussion, and vocal group called Giwayen Mata has been performing in Atlanta, Georgia. In 2013, the group hosted DanceAfrica Atlanta. This four-day event celebrated African music, dance, and culture. Choreographer and African dance teacher Chuck Davis founded DanceAfrica USA, the national organization that has put on the event annually since 1977. But Omelika Kuumba, Giwayen Mata's artistic director, is the driving force for bringing African dance to the mainstream dance community at the local level. She is also a bit of a pioneer in another way.

One of the things that makes Giwayen Mata different is that it is an all-female dance group. In its early years, the group faced some sexism. Traditional African dance enthusiasts thought that only men should be allowed to play the drums for African dance. Kuumba wanted to know why women and girls were not allowed to participate in the making of the music. She actually took the question to male drummers in Africa.

Their reasons varied. Some of the dancers thought that only men should drum simply because that was the way it had always been in the past. Men had played the drums while the women chose to dance along to the rhythms instead. Other dancers hinted that allowing women to drum was sacrilegious, as only male priests had traditionally been allowed to play the sacred *djembe* drum. And some even insisted that females could seriously hurt themselves by playing the drums if they didn't do it exactly right. Kuumba's teacher, Baba Atu Murray, maintained this belief.

Still, none of these reasons convinced Kuumba to give up her dream. African culture—particularly African dance—had been part of Kuumba's life since her childhood in the 1960s. She attended the first DanceAfrica festival in 1977 at the Brooklyn Academy of Music, where she saw Davis perform. She told *The Atlanta Journal-Constitution*, "Even if I didn't have an appreciation for African music and dance, I would have been excited just watching him, because of all the positive energy he emanates."

The respect that she still feels for Davis is definitely returned. He thinks highly of both Kuumba and her Giwayen Mata group. He was especially impressed with how well they all work together. "There was absolutely no cat-fighting and no egomaniacs on board," he told the publication. "These women knew exactly what they were doing and [were] into their music for the long haul. I also saw that Sister Omelika was respected, and thus the repertoire could grow by leaps and bounds."

The 2013 festival wasn't the first time that Giwayen Mata had performed with DanceAfrica. Davis invited the group to perform in three of its events in 2008. Giwayen Mata traveled to Chicago, Dallas, and Kuumba's old neighborhood of Brooklyn that year. They also returned to Brooklyn in 2013 for a repeat performance before holding the Atlanta event.

Giwayen Mata has attracted national attention from some pretty important people. Martin Luther King III was so impressed with their performances that he agreed to serve as an honorary chairperson for DanceAfrica Atlanta. His main role was assisting the group with fundraising for the event.

Even with Giwayen Mata's success in other states, Kuumba remains dedicated to keeping African dance a part of her local community. In 2011, she organized a community showcase for the people of Atlanta. It included about two dozen dancers from different African dance companies. Each group contributed a piece of choreography for a performance of *sinte*, a traditional rite-of-passage dance from Guinea. The group

A DanceAfrica performer rehearses at New York's Brooklyn Academy of Music before her official performance in "A Dancer's Path: Ancient Traditions, Modern Trends."

effort was part of what inspired her to help make DanceAfrica Atlanta a reality.

Kuumba shared with *The Atlanta Journal-Constitution*, "The energy was so wonderful. I felt we needed to do DanceAfrica, because Atlanta artists can come together . . . sharing this beautiful thing called African music and dance . . .

And I wanted to include Baba Chuck [Davis]. I wanted someone who had 'the light.'"

She hopes that the audience sees that light. She wants people to feel joy, excitement, and rejuvenation when the dancers perform. She told *The Atlanta Journal-Constitution* that her goal is "to feature companies that have been here with our noses to the grindstone for a while, and let, hopefully the country—and possibly the world—see what Atlanta has to offer."

It's not just professional dancers who can harness the power of African dance, however. People who may never set foot on a stage can also benefit from this powerful medium. Just ask Christa Fatou who leads an African dance class in Jacksonville, Florida. While other dance classes in the area rely on hip-hop music or house dance music to set the rhythm, Fatou's choice of dance, called lamba, is much older than these modern music styles. Instead, it is performed to the sound of drums.

"This lamba we're doing is from thirteenth century Mali, so it's one of the oldest rhythms," Fatou told *The Florida Times-Union*. "There's no way to know every single step that goes with it, because it's traveled so much." Fatou shared that the lamba is actually older than the drums themselves. "These instruments we're using, the djembe and the djun djun, are actually more modern forms of African instruments," she pointed out. "Originally, lamba wasn't even played on them. It was played on the balafon, which is the precursor to the xylophone."

Fatou and her business partner, Fhanta Williams, are professionals. In their day jobs, they lead the Nan Nkama West African Drum and Dance Ensemble. Fatou told *The Florida Times-Union* that the lamba classes attract a mix of people. "Some people come in as dancers, some people come in wanting a workout."

Outsiders' reactions to the class vary. People sometimes find the clothing a bit odd. For example, participants wear *lapas*, traditional dance skirts. Others assume that the dance

Women in Ghana prepare to perform at a community event wearing traditional clothing.

is an introduction into a religous cult. One of the participants, Kifimbo Parnell, reported to *The Florida Times-Union* that some people have shared this kind of suspicion with her. "When you tell them about dancing in bare feet and wearing a lapa, they're like: 'What is that? Is it voodoo? What are you guys doing over there?'"

To Fatou, however, sharing the dance with newcomers is a way of sharing her ancestry and its culture with others. As she told *The Florida Times-Union,* "When I was little, my mother did a lot to expose me to African culture. She'd say, 'When I hear those drums, I feel like I'm being called home.' So I was always attracted to it."

Williams told *The Florida Times-Union* that her father also raised her to appreciate African culture. "He gave us all African names and the history behind the names. He was a performer of martial arts himself . . . so the performing aspect was bred into me from the time I was five years old." She thinks that many people would enjoy the classes she and Fatou

The KanKouran West African Dance Company leaves its doors open during a community class. As the participants take part, onlookers sit and watch the activity.

offer—they just need to discover them. "I believe that by us being here with the windows open, letting them hear us drum, letting them hear us laugh, clap, all of that is probably resonating with the people outside. We just have to get out there and let them know that we're here."

Tammy Hall enjoys the classes immensely. "We all feel lifted after class," she shared with *The Florida Times-Union*. "It just embodies sisterhood and togetherness. I might not make it to the gym or YMCA, but I will come to African dance class. I like all the gyrating and the hip-shaking, but it has purpose. . . . You're showing your femininity and your power. You're embodying your grace as a woman, and you just have higher esteem about yourself."

For Kifimbo Parnell, the connection to lamba comes as much from the music as the movement. "The drums call me," she explained to *The Florida Times-Union*. "A week without it, you feel kind of like part of you is missing. I come here not just for the dance, but to connect with a continent that I might not ever see. This is Africa coming to me."

Preserving African Roots
Through Dance

Jennifer Stott moved to Provo, Utah, in 2004. One might not immediately think of this city—with a largely white, Mormon population—as being a hot spot for African culture. And it's true. When Stott arrived, there wasn't much in the way of African music or dance in the area. What she did find was that a large number of African American children had been adopted by white families in this part of the country. She wanted to give them access to their heritage. And she did so through dance.

Stott took action in 2006. She found an empty rehearsal space and began teaching nine children African dance and drumming. She named her group the Elikya Dance & Drum Company—*elikya* is Swahili for "hope." Today the company serves a total of thirty boys and girls.

One of them is Sage Service's daughter, Maya. Service told *The Salt Lake Tribune* that Maya's experience with the group has been an extremely positive one. "She gets a better sense of herself, plus it's every little girl's dream to perform. When they get together, it's like an unspoken understanding is at work. They can just be themselves. It's magical, really."

Stott wants the nonprofit group to serve a dual purpose. "I have two goals," she shared with *The Salt Lake Tribune*. "The first, most important, is for every girl to graduate from high school with honors and go on to college. The second is to show our culture to the entire state of Utah."

Several different cultures contribute to the Colombian dance tradition of cumbia. It has African and European as well as local influences. The unique blend of music, movement, and costumes is part of makes cumbia so popular.

Chapter 4
The Evolution of
African Dance

One of the most interesting trends in African dance is the merging of different cultures. Cumbia, for example, is a well-known traditional music and dance form in the country of Colombia. But it has African, European, and local influences. The African origins of the music are heard at once in the drums that give cumbia its rhythm. South American culture adds the sound of the flute to the music. And European influences can be heard in its melodies and seen in the costumes worn by dancers.

Although all three ethnic groups have helped to shape cumbia, the dance was created by African slaves. The Spaniards brought West Africans to Colombia's Caribbean coast during their seventeenth century colonization of the area. The word cumbia comes from the word *cumbe*, which is a type of dance from the African country of Guinea. Cumbia became especially popular during the 1950s and 60s. Today young people appear to be giving it new life, as more and more dancers are bringing it back into style.

The renewed interest in the dance has also created new interest in the music. Numerous popular musicians in Colombia, Mexico, and other Latin American countries have recorded cumbia music. Digital cumbia has become especially popular in Argentina in recent years. And in Colombia, musicians are fusing cumbia with modern music.

Mario Galeano heads the group Frente Cumbiero, a modern Colombian cumbia band. In an interview with *Sounds and Colours* newsletter, he explained, "It's very electric our sound. We have our thing with electric guitars, keyboards, and synthesisers. Even with the wind (sax and clarinet) we process them through a lot of effects so in the end the sound is very electric with the band. As we don't have singers we focus a lot on the dance floor, so people can get into dancing and don't have to look at the stage for the affirmation of the singer."

In traditional cumbia music, three different types of drums help make up the unique sounds. The deepest thuds come from a two-sided bass drum, known as the *tambora*. Drummers add backup rhythm with a mid-drum called the *tambor alegre*. And a calling drum—or *llamador*—provides the back-beat. Finally, these sounds are enhanced with *maracas* and *guaches*, which make rattling noises when shaken.

Three different types of Colombian flutes, or *gaitas*, are also used to create the sound of cumbia music. The first, called the *gaita macho*, provides rhythm and harmony. It is considered a masculine sound. The second, called the *gaita hembra*, provides a more feminine melody. The third flute, the *flauta de millo*, also helps carry the melody of the music. Although traditional cumbia music had no lyrics, modern versions match vocals to the music.

The traditional clothing worn by dancers is an important part of the dance itself. The men wear white shirts called *guayaberas*. They also wear hats on their heads and red handkerchiefs around their necks. A man may dance while taking his hat off or putting it on, or waving his handkerchief in the air. The woman's long flowing skirt, called a *pollera*, is used in sweeping motions, or even to hide her face in a playful way. She often dances while carrying a lit candle in one of her hands. Martin Vejarano teaches cumbia dance and music across the United States. He told *Dance Magazine* that traditional cumbia was used as a way for men to woo women. "It's a courtship dance. He's trying to conquer her heart."

Another cross-cultural dance experience is carnival. Combining African and local music and dance moves, the most

Samba dancing is an important part of Brazilian carnival. The dance was developed by former African slaves in the late nineteenth century. It didn't become popular until the twentieth century, though.

famous carnivals take place in Brazil and the island country of Trinidad and Tobago. A similar event can also be seen each year on the streets of England. People of Afro-Caribbean heritage celebrate their history by dancing in the streets in colorful costumes at the Notting Hill Carnival. This street festival, the largest in Europe, is based on nineteenth century carnivals that were held in the Caribbean to celebrate abolition, the ending of slavery in that region. The European version of the celebration has taken place each year since 1964.

Local versions of the Trinidad and Tobago Carnival also take place annually in major cities across the United States. Adorned with feathers, jewels, and masks, paraders dance in the streets to the sounds of soca music. This form of music developed in Trinidad and Tobago from the West African kaiso music that was brought to the country by slaves. Today, the music and the dance associated with it are making their way into dance and fitness classes in the US and abroad.

Michael Burgess is a professional dancer from Belize who trained at the Alvin Ailey American Dance Theater in New York. While there he studied African contemporary, flamenco, and other types of cross-cultural dance. When he attended the Harlem School of Arts, his interest in West African dance deepened. He was especially interested in dance forms practiced in Ghana, Guinea, and Senegal. He told *The Times*, "A lot of the dancing you see at carnival originates from West African countries, but the basic squat position is more Senegalese. You are working your bum; it is very earthy, grounded, rooted."

Burgess also teaches this form of dancing as a type of fitness as well as fun. He calls his class "Carnival Slam." The pastime delivers an intense workout. Participants can burn more than four hundred calories during a single class. At the same time, you don't have to be a talented athlete to take part. "Carnival is all about letting go, and I want to help people to do that." Burgess told *Daily Mail* reporter Alice Von Simson, who attended one of his classes. "We are going to learn a few moves today but the point is that it's supposed to be fun so if you miss a step, or don't remember what you're supposed to be doing, just make it up."

The more you practice the moves taught in classes like Carnival Slam, the more coordinated you will get. And you might get so caught up in the fun, you don't even notice how hard you are working. Von Simson said that the class began with a warmup like most fitness classes do. "But even this was exciting," she added, "because of all the drumming."

Von Simson thoroughly enjoyed the experience all the way to the end. "I hate to say this," she confided, "but about halfway through I started to wonder if perhaps the Carnival Slam class was a teeny bit more fun than the Carnival itself . . . I left the class with a whole set of new dancing skills and the confidence to get out there and express myself."

When many people think of African dance, they only consider traditional African forms. But modern African dance includes many styles—including ballet. This dance form requires a great deal of athleticism and discipline. And for boys, it can sometimes require a thick skin. South African dancer Andile Ndlovu found this out firsthand when he began dancing as a boy. Ndlovu grew up in Soweto, a rough neighborhood of Johannesburg. His friends didn't seem to understand his love of dance. "I used to be picked upon for the way I walk and the way I act or carry myself," he told CNN, adding that he became known as "the dude who did ballet."

Even his close friends teased him about his choice to pursue the pastime. They not only teased him for the dancing itself, but also for the clothing and shoes he had to wear when practicing and performing. But Ndlovu didn't let their words stop him from pursuing his dreams. He had already overcome the South African stereotype that ballet was for wealthy, white dancers. In 2008, he was offered a spot at The Washington Ballet dance company in the United States. His success there helped him go on to win awards in international ballet competitions in Boston and in Cape Town back in South Africa.

"What I wanted was to change people's minds in South Africa about black ballet dancers," he told CNN. "I wanted to change that view, because everybody used to put it in a category for the elite people or, you know, it's only for a certain racial group. I [want to] set the bar for anybody else that's coming, that's growing up, that's coming behind, and they will learn from my actions and what I do and hopefully I become a role model for them, especially South Africans."

In 2013, these men in Kenya performed a traditional dance with drums. Drumming is a key element of African dance. It also provides an intense physical workout to participants.

Chapter 5
Moving to the Beat of Different Drums

Many African dance forms rely heavily on drumming. The speed and style of the movements are based on the rhythms from these powerful instruments. For some, though, the drumming *is* actually the dance. And it can be a fun and challenging workout.

Drumming classes have spread from the African continent to other parts of the world, where this pastime is a relatively new one. Steve Bedford, who lives in Warwick, England, attended a West African drumming class at the Sydni Centre in nearby Sydenham. He told the *Coventry Evening Telegraph*, "I found out about the drumming while surfing on the Internet. I had done some DJing and a few evening courses in music and I used to do fencing but it got to the point where it wasn't doing it for me so I started looking for another activity."

Drumming definitely has much to offer someone looking to add something new to their fitness routine. Bedford's class was based on the drumming of the Malinke, an ethnic group found in the countries of Guinea and Mali. Participants use a variety of drums to create a polyrhythmic sound. They may drum while sitting or standing. Either way, the drumming quickly becomes a cardiovascular activity. It involves constant upper-body movement. This type of exercise has many health benefits. It improves balance and coordination as well as core stability. It also reduces stress, which is something Bedford was hoping to gain from a new fitness routine.

"I went along to the drumming and was quite nervous at first but everyone was very welcoming and within five minutes of walking through the door I had a drum between my legs and was banging away," he told the *Coventry Evening Telegraph*. "You can pick up the basics pretty easily, and if you take it at the right pace, which is what this class does, then it's great. . . . I have found I'm much more relaxed generally, I feel much better, my fitness has improved, and there is a real difference in the shape of my upper body because of the effort I put in with the drums."

A school in Liverpool, England, gives young people a chance to try drumming firsthand. It also teaches them about the different origins of the activity. When Rice Lane Junior School first offered a drumming class, the response was tremendous. So many students signed up that the school had to divide the program into two sessions.

Pauline Doyle is the school's deputy head. She reported to the *Liverpool Echo* that the kids enjoyed several benefits from the class. In addition to being a great fitness activity, the drumming boosted the participants' self-esteem and exposed them to a new type of music. She pointed out that it is *not* a quiet activity, however. "The children loved it and at times it was so loud our teeth were rattling. We were careful that exams were not on at the same time."

Even with all the clamor, though, the learning continued. "The sessions are not just about drumming. During the six-week programme at the school there is a geography context look at both Brazil and the African origins of drumming," Doyle explained to the *Liverpool Echo*. "The children are shown a slide show so they can see different cultures, carnivals, and how the drumming has evolved."

Classes that offer African drumming and dancing can also be found in the United States on both coasts. They are even becoming more popular in the Midwest, slowly. Gordon Kay is a drummer who works alongside instructor Djibril Camara in Urbana, Illinois. "It's becoming more common for West African dancers to come here and teach, but they're still heavily located on the West Coast and in the East," he told *The News*

Drumming can be a confidence-boosting activity for young people. It can also be a lot of fun.

Gazette. He added, "There are not many college towns in the Midwest that have as skilled of a dancer as Djibi."

Camara has also taught at the University of Illinois and performed in various area schools and festivals. Before he began teaching, he was a professional dancer for twenty years. He spent the bulk of those years as the principal dancer and choreographer for Ballet du Afrique Noir. This dance company toured Africa, Europe, and the United States.

The enjoyment Camara gets from teaching shows in his smile as he leads his ninety-minute class. Despite its length and intensity, he manages to keep the students enthralled. Heather Ault told *The News Gazette*, "The drummers and dancers are always talking to one another and synchronized with one another."

Fellow student Amy Swanson added, "It provides a ton of energy for the dancers. That's what's great about this class."

Guinea native Djibril Camara is a West African dance master. Through his class at the Channing-Murray Foundation, he brings the art of West African dance to the people of Urbana, Illinois.

Still, the intensity of the pastime cannot be denied. Using the whole body, the movements are large and lively. At the end of the session, which offers no breaks, the dancers form a large circle. Each dancer then takes a turn dancing in its center while the others clap.

Jamie McGowan is the associate director of the University of Illinois's Center for African Studies. She told *The News Gazette,* "It's a great workout, and it's a lot of fun, and he's always throwing in new steps so you can't get bored."

At the end of the class, student Ann-Marie Shapiro is both exhausted and happy. "I had to join a gym so I could work out so I could do this once a week," she revealed to The *News Gazette.* But she clearly doesn't mind. "It's so fun. There's nothing else like it that I've ever done that makes me as joyful as this."

If you are interested in studying African dance, you may not even realize that you already have some useful skills. Chances are good that other dance classes you have attended taught you at least a few movements you will use in African dance. Although many African dance classes cater to beginners, if you have never taken any kind of dance class, you might want to start with ballet. Many dance teachers recommend starting with this dance form, especially if you'd like to dance professionally.

Tiffany Barnes is the director of the Ailey School's Junior Division in New York. She explained to *Backstage* magazine, "It doesn't mean that we are preparing every student to be a ballet dancer, but the basis for performing professionally in many different dance styles involves being well-trained in ballet." Students at the Ailey School continue ballet training along with another type of dance—such as hip-hop, Spanish, tap, or West African dance—up until the age of seventeen.

Barnes also shared that studying music is an important part of learning dance as well. The Ailey School encourages its students to learn how to sing or play a musical instrument. For a person interested in studying traditional African dance, the drums seem an ideal instrument choice.

Even if you never plan to pursue African dance professionally, you still may want to think about sampling these other aspects of the dance and music worlds. Taking a class or learning to play an instrument is never a waste of time. Anything you can do to become a better dancer will surely help you enjoy the pastime even more.

Check with local dance studios or health clubs to see if they offer classes in African dance or drumming. If they don't, suggest that they consider adding one. You can also search online for "African dance" in your area to see if there are studios that specialize in this form of dance.

If your school has a music program, ask the teacher if he or she would consider adding African dance and drumming to the course program. In African dance, music and dance are deeply linked. Learning one will almost certainly involve the other.

Check with your local library to see if it has any books or videos on African dance. Joneeba, for example, can be learned this way.

Research different types of African dance, and explore different classes. With thousands of cultures on the African continent, there are countless types of African dance. If you don't enjoy the first one you try, feel free to try others!

Ask your friends if they would enjoy learning African dance with you. Nearly every type of dance is more fun with other people. This is especially true of African dance, which traditionally has been performed in groups.

1500s–1700s	Millions of African people are captured and shipped to the New World; Europeans begin the practice of "dancing the slaves" to keep slaves healthy on ships. Capoeira, a dance combined with martial arts, begins to develop in Brazil. Cumbia begins to develop in Colombia.
1800s	Carnivals are held in the Caribbean to celebrate abolition.
1830s	Minstrel shows become popular.
1840s	William Henry Lane performs in minstrel shows; Lane goes on tour with an all-white American dance company as its star.
1861–1865	The US Civil War.
1890s	Brazil outlaws capoeira.
1930s	Brazilian President Getúlio Vargas legalizes capoeira.
1950s	Cumbia becomes popular again in Colombia.
1964	The first Notting Hill Carnival takes place in London; it becomes an annual event.
1969	Arthur Mitchell and Karel Shook found the Dance Theatre of Harlem.
1977	The first DanceAfrica festival is held at the Brooklyn Academy of Music.
1993	Giwayen Mata is formed.
2001	Djoniba Mouflet publishes a book which describes his African dance technique called Joneeba.
2006	Jennifer Stott opens the Elikya Dance & Drum Company.
2008	Giwayen Mata performs with DanceAfrica in Chicago, Dallas, and New York.
2011	Naomi Fall and Mohamed Coulibaly open their dance studio called GnagamiX in Africa.
2013	Point Park University holds World Cultural Dance Week in Pittsburgh, Pennsylvania.
2014	Bakomanga, a music and dance group from Madagascar, comes to the United States for the first time to perform in DanceAfrica.

Books

Glass, Barbara S. *African American Dance: An Illustrated History*. Jefferson, NC: McFarland, 2012.

Hanley, Elizabeth A. et al. *African Dance*. New York: Chelsea House, 2010.

Mouflet, Djoniba. *Joneeba!* New York: Hatherleigh Press, 2001.

Welsh-Asante, Kariamu, ed. *African Dance: An Artistic, Historical, and Philosophical Inquiry*. Trenton, NJ: Africa World Press, Inc., 1998.

DVDs

Bono, Debra. *African Dance Workout*. Hackensack, NJ: Bayview Entertainment/Widowmaker, 2008.

Forbes-Vierling, Suzanne. *Tribal Energy Cardio*. San Diego, CA: Tribal Energy.

Mouflet, Djoniba. *Joneeba*. New York: Djoniba Dance & Drum Centre, 2005.

Nuamah, Kukuwa. *Kukuwa Dance Workout*. Orland Park, IL: MPI Home Video, 2005.

Wyoma. *African Healing Dance*. Louisville, CO: Sounds True, 1998.

Works Consulted

Curnow, Robyn, and Eoghan Macguire. "South African Ballet Dancer Confounds Stereotypes." CNN, November 22, 2011. http://www.cnn.com/2011/11/22/world/africa/av-andile-ndlovu/index.html

Dacko, Karen. "Making It Happen: Pittsburgh Goes Global." *Dance Magazine,* July 2013.

Discover Colombia! "Cumbia: The Rhythm of Colombia." http://discovercolombia.com/cumbia-the-rhythm-of-colombia/

Fall, Naomi. "Why I Dance: Naomi Fall." *Dance Magazine,* July 2013.

Fulton, Ben. "Elikya Dance & Drum Company: African Culture in Motion." *Salt Lake Tribune*, January 6, 2012.

Hambridge, Karen. "Getting Fit Has Never Been So Much Fun." *Coventry Evening Telegraph*, January 7, 2008.

Kirsch, Michele. "Shaking It Like a Real Carnival Queen." *Times (London, UK)*, August 23, 2008.

Merli, Melissa. "Dancing to Drumming—and Vice Versa: West African Traditional-Dance Class a Full-Body, Soul Experience." *News-Gazette (East Central Illinois)*, March 12, 2009.

Mosley, Sydnie L. "Teacher's Wisdom: Djoniba Mouflet." *Dance Magazine*, June 2011, Volume 85, Issue 6.

The Notting Hill Carnival. "History." http://www.thenottinghillcarnival.com/history/

Perry, Cynthia Bond. "Finding Their Own Rhythm: Atlantan Grows with African Dance Group. Ensemble Giwayen Mata Comes Full Circle to Host 4-Day Festival." *Atlanta Journal-Constitution*, June 7, 2013.

Sagolla, Lisa Jo. "Dance Training for Children and Teens." *Backstage*, March 23, 2011, Volume 52, Issue 12.

Sciurba, Katie. "Dance . . . Fight . . . Play . . . Capoeira!" *Faces*, February 2009, Volume 25, Issue 5.

Slater, Russ. "We Don't Need the Mainstream: An Interview with Frente Cumbiero's Mario Galeano." *Sounds and Colours*, December 5, 2011. http://www.soundsandcolours.com/articles/colombia/ we-dont-need-the-mainstream-an-interview-with-frente-cumbieros-mario-galeano/

Traiger, Lisa. "'JUBA!' Celebrates Tap's Old Master." *Washington Post*, December 7, 2012.

Turner, Ben. "Drumming up Fun: Brazilian Beats Aiding Fitness and Self-Esteem." *Liverpool Echo*, January 19, 2010.

Von Simson, Alice. "Shake It Like a Carnival Queen and Get in Shape with This New Fitness Craze." *Daily Mail*, August 12, 2008. http://www.dailymail.co.uk/femail/article-1043566/Shake-like-carnival-queen-shape-new-fitness-craze.html

Weathersbee, Tonyaa. "West African Dance Classes a Celebration of Culture and Kinship." *Florida Times-Union*, May 16, 2011.

Wisner, Heather. "Cumbia: The New/Old Latin Dance." *Dance Magazine*, September 2006.

On the Internet

Frente Cumbiero
    http://www.frentecumbiero.com/hola/DubMeCrazy/

Kukuwa Dance Workout
    http://www.kukuwadanceworkout.com/

"Sissan Dédo! De Pierre Doussaint pour GnagamiX." YouTube video, 10:16. Posted by "GnagamiX Danse," October 31, 2013. http://www.youtube.com/watch?v=X1Ct24IJz9U

Start Playing Capoeira: "A Brief History of Capoeira"
    http://www.start-playing-capoeira.com/history-of-capoeira.html

"Traditional Dancing in Cartagena, Colombia—Cumbia." YouTube video, 5:03. Posted by "MrPiettu," September 17, 2011. http://www.youtube.com/watch?v=QcLSK9mv_mA

West African Dance with Youssouf Koumbassa
    http://westafricandance.com/

World Arts West: "West African Dance"
    http://www.worldartswest.org/plm/guide/locator/westafrican.shtml

abolition (ab-uh-LISH-uhn)—The legal ending of slavery.

choreography (kohr-ee-OG-ruh-fee)—The art of composing dances and planning their movements.

contemporary dance (kuhn-TEMP-puh-rer-ee DANS)—A style of dance which incorporates many styles of dance such as classical ballet and modern dance.

discipline (DIS-uh-plin)—Behavior and order maintained by training and control.

ethnomusicology (eth-noh-myoo-zi-KOL-uh-jee)—The study of music around the world, its development, and its relationship to the cultures to which it belongs.

phonetic (fuh-NET-ik)—Written in a way that corresponds to pronunciation.

polyrhythmic (pol-ee-RITH-mik)—Having simultaneous, sharply contrasting rhythms within a composition.

precarious (pri-KAIR-ee-uhs)—Unstable, dangerous.

primitive (PRIM-i-tiv)—Characteristic of an early state of human development; uncivilized.

recreation (rek-ree-EY-shuhn)—An activity which is done for relaxation and enjoyment.

repertoire (REP-er-twahr)—The list of pieces that a company performs.

sacrilegious (sak-ruh-LIJ-uhs)—Violating something that is considered sacred.

segregated (SEG-ri-gey-tid)—Having separate facilities for members of different races or other groups.

stereotype (STER-ee-oh-tahyp)—A standard conception or image commonly held about an entire group of people.

Swahili (swah-HEE-lee)—The language spoken by the Swahili people, found on the coast of East Africa.

uncivilized (uhn-SIV-uh-lahyzd)—Not cultured, wild, savage.

voodoo (VOO-doo)—A West African religion which is based on a belief in many gods and spirits, and features rituals involving music and dance.

PHOTO CREDITS: All design elements from Thinkstock/Sharon Beck; Cover, p. 1—Photos.com/Thinkstock; pp. 4-5, 16, 21, 29; pp. 6, 8—Library of Congress; p. 11—Public Domain; p. 12—Hans Nathan; pp. 14, 22—Getty Images; pp. 19, 41—Anke Van Wyk/Dreamstime; p. 20—Michele Alfieri/Dreamstime; p. 25—Richard Termine/AP Images; p. 27—USAID Africa Bureau; pp. 28, 35—The Washington Post/Getty Images; p. 30—Dreamstime; p. 33—Willy Setiadi/Dreamstime; p. 36—Dr Ajay Kumar Singh/Dreamstime; p. 39—Frances Fruit/Dreamstime; p. 40—Robert K. O'Daniel/The News-Gazette/AP Images; p. 42—Roger Mcclean/Dreamstime

Index

About the Author

Tammy Gagne is the author of numerous books for adults and children, including *Trends in Martial Arts* and *We Visit South Africa* for Mitchell Lane Publishers. She resides in northern New England with her husband and son. One of her favorite pastimes is visiting schools to speak to kids about the writing process.

Per RFP 03764 Follett School Solutions guarantees
hardcover bindings through SY 2024-2025
877.899.8550 or customerservice@follett.com